RAINBOW magic®

The Green Fairies

For Isabelle Hudson,
with lots of love

Special thanks to
Sue Mongredien

ORCHARD BOOKS
338 Euston Road, London NW1 3BH
Orchard Books Australia
Level 17/207 Kent Street, Sydney, NSW 2000

A Paperback Original
First published in 2009 by Orchard Books.

A CIP catalogue record for this book is available
from the British Library.

ISBN 978 1 40830 475 4

9 10

Printed in Great Britain

The paper and board used in this paperback are natural recyclable
products made from wood grown in sustainable forests. The
manufacturing processes conform to the environmental regulations
of the country of origin.

Orchard Books is a division of Hachette Children's Books,
an Hachette UK company

Isabella
the Air Fairy

by Daisy Meadows

ORCHARD

The fairies must be in a dream
If they think they can be called "green".
My goblin servants are definitely greenest
And I, of course, am by far the meanest.

Seven fairies out to save the Earth?
This idea fills me with mirth!
I'm sure the world has had enough
Of fairy magic and all that stuff.

So I'm going to steal the fairies' wands
And send them into human lands.
The fairies will think all is lost
Defeated again, by me, Jack Frost!

Contents

Flower Fairy   9

All of a Flutter!   19

Goblin Alert   31

Lots of Butterflies   41

Get That Wand!   51

Tickle, Tickle!   61

Flower Fairy

"Rachel! Kirsty! Hurry up, we need to go!" came a voice from downstairs.

"Coming, Mum!" Kirsty Tate shouted back, putting her hair in a ponytail. "There," she said. "Are you ready, Rachel?"

Rachel Walker, Kirsty's best friend, frowned as she gazed around the bedroom the two girls were sharing. "Nearly," she said. "I don't know where my shoes are. Have you seen them?"

Kirsty shook her head. "Maybe they're in the hall?" she suggested.

The girls hurried down to find their parents waiting by the front door. The two families were staying in a cottage together for a week on Rainspell Island… a very magical place, as Kirsty and Rachel had discovered the first time they'd been there for a holiday. That had certainly been a summer to remember: not only had they met each other, but they'd also met some other very special friends – fairy friends!

So far, this holiday was proving to be just as exciting. They'd only arrived yesterday but Rachel and Kirsty had soon found themselves in another wonderful fairy adventure, this time helping the Green Fairies in a mission to clean up the world's environmental problems.

Today, the two families were going to Seabury, a town on the mainland. The girls wanted to see a film at the cinema and the grown-ups were going shopping. Kirsty and Rachel really hoped they'd meet another fairy at some point!

Mr Walker looked at his watch. "Girls, we have to leave now if you're going to catch the start of the film.

The ferry to the mainland goes in ten minutes, and there's not another one for an hour after that."

"I can't find my shoes, Dad," Rachel said, hunting all over the cloakroom. "Oh, where could they be?"

Kirsty helped her look and the girls searched the entire cottage before finally finding the shoes under Rachel's bed.

"At last," said Mr Tate when they reappeared. "We'll have to drive to the ferry port now, rather than walk. We're already cutting it fine."

The two families got into the Tates' car and drove off. They arrived at the port just in time. They took the car onto the ferry, and, moments later, the ferry sailed across to Seabury. It was only a short journey and, before long, the two families were back in the car and driving into the little town.

It was very busy. A huge traffic jam snaked back from the main shopping street, and the cars crawled along a metre at a time.

"Ugh," Kirsty said, closing her window. "What a smell!"

"It's the fumes from the traffic," her mum said, wrinkling her nose as an old car went by, pumping stinky grey smoke from its exhaust.

"I don't know where we're going to park," Mr Tate sighed, leaning against the steering wheel. "I wish we hadn't brought the car, we'd have been much quicker walking."

Rachel bit her lip. It was her fault they were in the car – if only she'd been able to find her shoes more quickly!

It took ages for the two families to find a car park with any spaces. "At last," Mrs Tate said, when they were finally able to walk into town. "I think you've missed the start of the film you wanted, girls, but there should be other films showing that you can see. There's the cinema at the end of the road, look. We'll pick you up in the foyer at four o'clock, OK?"

The girls said goodbye to their parents and headed off, chatting about other films they could watch instead.

Just before they reached the cinema, they passed a shop which had big tubs of flowers outside. "Look at these grey flowers," Kirsty remarked. "They're very unusual. I've never seen grey flowers before, have you?"

Rachel stroked one of the oval petals lightly. To her surprise, the grey came off on her thumb, leaving a streaky white colour underneath! "They're not grey," Rachel said. "It's just the pollution that's made them *look* grey."

Kirsty gently rubbed at another petal. That one had a thin film of grey over it too. "Poor flowers," she said. "Where has all the dirt come from?"

Before Rachel could reply, she saw something glittering at the back of the flower arrangement…and then, in a flurry of sparkles, out popped a tiny fairy. It was Isabella the Air Fairy!

All of a Flutter!

Isabella had long brown hair that tumbled about her shoulders. She wore a floaty purple dress with a bright golden belt around it, and cropped jeans underneath. Kirsty and Rachel were delighted to see her again.

"Hello!" they chorused. They had been friends with the fairies for a long time now, but it was still so exciting to have adventures with a new fairy.

"Hello," Isabella said in a tinkly voice. "Kirsty and Rachel, isn't it? I met you yesterday."

"That's right," Kirsty said. She and Rachel had visited Fairyland to ask for the king and queen's help with improving the environment. There, they had met seven fairies, who were in training to earn their magic wands. The fairies were called Nicole, Isabella, Edie, Coral, Lily, Milly and Carrie.

The king and queen had set the fairies
a challenge – they were to become the
"Green Fairies" for a trial period, to help
humans with environmental issues, like
pollution and littering. Kirsty and Rachel
knew that if this trial period was
successful, the king and queen would
make the Green Fairies permanent!

"Hi, Isabella," Rachel said now. "Have
you found your wand yet? Or can we
help you look for it?"

Isabella smiled. "Thank you," she
replied. "No, I haven't seen my wand
anywhere. And I really
need it so that I can
begin my assignment.
It's my job to clean up
the air, and the sooner
I can start, the better!"

Kirsty nodded, her eyes flicking to the grimy grey petals of the flowers nearby. "This place certainly needs cleaning," she said. "Well, we helped Nicole find her wand yesterday, and we've promised to help all the other Green Fairies do the same. We can't let Jack Frost get away with his mean tricks!"

Jack Frost was always up to no good. This time, he'd appeared just as the seven Green Fairies had been about to start the Wand Ceremony, in which they would each receive a special wand to help them with their work. Bertram, a

22

friendly frog footman, had been holding
the seven wands, when suddenly Jack
Frost's goblin servants had turned up,
snatched them all and then vanished.
"My goblins are the only real green
creatures!" Jack Frost had sneered. "And
I don't want any silly fairies interfering!"
And then he'd disappeared too, before
anyone could stop him.

The goblins were hiding in the human
world with the wands,
and Kirsty and
Rachel had
vowed to track
them down.

"I know roughly
where the goblin
with my wand is,"
Isabella told the girls now.

"So if you don't mind coming on a little journey with me…"

"We'd love to!" Kirsty said at once.

Isabella grinned. "I was hoping you'd say that," she said.

"We have to be back to meet our parents at four o'clock," Rachel reminded her friends.

"That's fine," said Isabella. She took a deep breath. "I think I have enough power to turn you into fairies for the trip." She waved her hands and a shower of shimmering blue fairy dust streamed from them, swirling all over the

girls. As soon as the magic sparkles
touched Kirsty and Rachel, they began
to shrink smaller and smaller.

"We're fairies!" Rachel said
excitedly, as she became
the same size as
Isabella. She flapped
her gauzy wings,
smiling as she
floated off
the ground.

"You certainly
are," Isabella said.
"And now that you're
ready…off we go!"
She waved her hands again and
a glittery swirl spun up from out
of nowhere, lifting the three of them
into the air and carrying them away.

Kirsty felt tingly. Another fairy adventure was beginning – hurrah!

A few moments later, they landed gently. Kirsty and Rachel looked around, and realised that they were perched on the roof of a building in the next town inland from Seabury. Below them was a mass of thick clouds, which was impossible to see through. "It's very foggy here," Rachel said.

Isabella looked sad. "That's not fog," she replied. "It's clouds of smog – dirty, smoky air. Doesn't it smell awful?"

Kirsty nodded. "It's horrible," she said. "It's making my throat hurt."

Just then, a tiny grey butterfly fluttered by. Seeing the fairies, she gave an excited squeak and zipped towards them...but then her antennae drooped. "Oh," she said, sounding disappointed.

"I thought you were butterflies like me. What kind of insect are *you*?"

"We're fairies," Isabella said, and introduced them all. "Who are you – and what are you doing all the way up here?"

"I'm Flutter," said the butterfly. "I'm fed up of living in the dirty city and so I'm looking for a nice green home and some other butterflies to live with. I haven't had any luck so far, though."

A tear rolled down her face and splashed onto the roof. "And now I'm lost. Please will you help me?"

Goblin Alert

"Of course we'll help," Isabella told the sad butterfly.

"Don't worry," Kirsty said. "We'll find you a home. Come on, let's fly down to the ground. There must be a nice park or bit of woodland…or even somebody's garden that would suit you."

The three fairies and Flutter set off, diving down through the air. It was hard work, flying through the clouds. Some were white and fluffy as usual, but others were grey and smelly with pollution. Rachel made the mistake of flying through one of the dirty clouds and came out coughing and choking, her eyes streaming. "Yuck!" she spluttered. "That was disgusting!"

They could see the ground beneath them now, and it was clear that they were in a much bigger town than Seabury.

There were lots of cars on the roads, and none actually seemed to be moving, as they were all stuck in a huge traffic jam. Flying nearer, Kirsty noticed that many cars only had one person inside.

Isabella was sighing unhappily. "If only humans could fly, like us fairies!" she said. "No wonder the air is so bad here! If some of those drivers shared their cars, or walked or cycled instead of driving everywhere, there would be less traffic on the road, and less pollution."

Kirsty nodded. She was starting to
realise that pollution affected everyone
and was *caused* by everyone, too. "We
must get our bikes out later this week,"
she vowed to Rachel. "We could go for
a family cycle ride around the coves!"

"Good idea," Rachel said. Then her
face brightened. "Oh – there's some
green down there," she said pointing.
"Let's fly down to see if we can find
a home for Flutter."

Flutter
wriggled her
antennae,
looking happier.
"Oh yes!" she
squeaked.
"Come on, let's
check it out!"

The four of them fluttered lower and
lower. As they got closer to the patch
of green, they realised that it was a
park – perfect. But then Kirsty frowned.
Maybe it wasn't so perfect after all.

"There's a big cloud over the park,"
she noticed. She wrinkled her nose and
fanned the air in front of her face. "And it
smells really strong – like nasty perfume!"

As they zoomed in
closer, they saw
who had made
the cloud. "It's
one of Jack
Frost's goblins!"
Rachel hissed,
landing on a
branch of a nearby tree
and peering at him. "What is he *doing*?"

The goblin had a can of air freshener in each hand and was spraying them up into the air. Around his waist, he wore a belt, onto which were attached even more cans of air freshener. He looked rather like a cowboy, Kirsty thought. Then her eyes widened as she saw what else was strapped to his belt. "Rachel, Isabella, look!" she hissed excitedly. "On his belt – it's Isabella's magic wand!"

"Well spotted!" Isabella cried.

Rachel bit her lip. "I can't believe the goblin is here in the middle of the park, in broad daylight, with a magic wand!" she whispered. "If someone spots him, it'll be a disaster!"

Flutter looked from one fairy to another, not understanding. "Why?" she asked. "Who is this person anyway?"  She coughed. "And why does he keep spraying that horrid stuff around? It smells awful!"

"He's a goblin. If humans get to know about Fairyland and all the magical people who live there, then the fairies will be in danger," Kirsty said. "People might try to catch them and put them in zoos or museums…it would be terrible."

Isabella shivered at the words, her wings trembling. "Don't!" she begged. "We can't let that happen. Thank goodness this part of the park seems empty and there's no one around to see him." She turned to Flutter. "In answer to your other question, the goblin stole my magic wand. I've got no idea why he's spraying

those cans, though. Maybe I should
ask him."

And with that, the little fairy swooped
impulsively from the branch and flew
straight towards the goblin.

Lots of Butterflies

Kirsty, Rachel followed their fairy friend.

"Hey!" Isabella called out. She was hovering a safe distance from the goblin, her hands on her hips. "What on earth are you doing, spraying all that air freshener around?"

The goblin puffed out his chest. "I'm being green, of course," he said. "I'm sorting out air pollution by making the air fresh."

Isabella stared at him. "No, you've got it all wrong," she said. "People use air freshener inside buildings – to cover up a bad smell." She folded her arms across her chest. "Although, frankly, they should just open a window. That's a much better way to clear the air."

The goblin looked scornful. "You're the one who's got it wrong," he said. "I'm a good reader, me, and I know what it says on these cans: Air Freshener." He pointed at each word as he read it, and a rather pleased expression appeared on his face.

"My plan is working very well," he said loftily. "The air smells really nice now."

Isabella narrowed her eyes. "But with all that spraying you've done, you've released hundreds of chemicals into the air. And those same chemicals will eventually soak down into the earth – did you think about that? They might do terrible damage to the soil and plants. And it'll be your fault!"

The goblin looked huffy. "Keep your nose out of my business," he warned. "Or I'll make *you* smell a bit nicer!" And he aimed the can straight at the fairies, and ran towards them, spraying out clouds of air freshener in their direction!

"Quick!" Rachel yelled. "Take cover!"

She and her friends dived into a nearby hedgerow, where the leaves would protect them from the spray.

"The chemicals in that stuff could damage our wings," Isabella said anxiously, checking them all over. "Honestly! That goblin is such a pest!"

"Yes, he's a nuisance, isn't he?" came a little voice just then. The three fairies and Flutter turned…and Flutter let out a gasp of delight.

There was a whole crowd of butterflies just behind them, all with brightly coloured wings and friendly faces!

"Hello," said a butterfly with pale yellow wings at the front of the pack.

"Well done for trying to stop that green chap. He's been spraying those cans all day — that's why we're hiding in here." She wiggled her antennae at Flutter. "Haven't seen you around here before. My name's Goldie. And this is Shimmer, Flit, Willow…"

Flutter was delighted to meet all the butterflies, and bobbed a happy little hello to each of them. "I'm Flutter, and this is Isabella, Rachel and Kirsty. Oh, it's wonderful to see all of you!" she cried. "I've been so lonely."

"It's nice to meet you too," smiled Flit, who had striking red and blue markings. "Aren't you an unusual colour? I've never seen a grey butterfly before."

Flutter's antennae drooped. "My wings look really boring next to all of yours," she said in a small voice. "I wish I was colourful too." A cornflower-blue butterfly put a kindly wing around Flutter. "I think your grey wings are very stylish," she said. "You are unique, my dear."

"Yes, it must be lovely to be different," said Goldie. "There are loads of us

yellows but you're the only grey I've ever seen. Will you stay with us for a while, Flutter? You'd be very welcome. This park is usually a lovely place to live – although not at the moment, unfortunately. What *is* that green fellow doing?"

They peeked out to see that the goblin was still squirting air freshener up into the sky, in big fragrant clouds.

The smell caught in Rachel's nose and she let out a sneeze. "Aaaaah-choo! We've really got to stop him," she said. "But how?"

Get That Wand!

The three fairies fell silent, each trying to think up a plan of action. As she racked her brain for a good idea, Kirsty realised that the goblin had gone quiet too. She peered out at him and saw that he was shaking his air freshener cans, then scowling and throwing them down on the ground. "They're empty," she realised aloud. "He's run out of the spray!"

The friends watched as the goblin tried each can in turn, but there was nothing left in any of them. The goblin wasn't happy and kicked out at the empty cans. Then he took the wand from his belt and tried waving it over the pile. "Magic yourselves full again!" he commanded – but nothing happened.

"This is our chance," Rachel whispered to Kirsty and Isabella. "He can't threaten us with the air freshener if it's all gone. Maybe we can snatch that wand away before he works out how to use it!"

"I agree," said Isabella. "Come on, we'll try to surprise him."

The fairies zoomed out of the hedge towards the goblin. A look of panic came over his face and he brandished the wand at them. "Freeze!" he commanded, but once again, nothing happened. He shook the wand irritably. "Always works when Jack Frost says it," he grumbled to himself. "Work, you stupid wand! Freeze those fairies!"

Isabella arched an eyebrow. "What *he* doesn't know is that a fairy's wand can never be used to do harm," she whispered to Kirsty and Rachel. "So don't worry. He won't be able to cast any freezing magic over us – or any other horrible spells either!" She grinned. "Let's try and grab it."

"If Kirsty and I whizz around his head, maybe he'll be distracted, and you can take the wand, Isabella," Rachel suggested.

"Good thinking," Kirsty said.

Kirsty and Rachel began zooming around the goblin, both in different directions, so that he went cross-eyed, trying to keep up with them. "Can't catch me!" Rachel giggled as she whooshed over one of his big green ears.

The goblin swiped at them, trying to bat them away with his big hands.

"Gerroff!" he yelled, sounding grumpy. "You just watch it or...or..." He scratched his head, trying to think of a threat.

"Or I'll tickle you with this wand!" He flourished it in mid air. "Yeah – that's what I'll do. Goblins are very ticklish – I bet fairies are as well."

He began jabbing the wand at them, as if he were a swordfighter, trying to tickle them with the end of it.

Then, as he thrust the wand out, Isabella suddenly caught hold of the other end of it, and clung on with all her might. "Help me," she called to Kirsty and Rachel. "We can pull it out of his grasp!"

Rachel and Kirsty flew to help their friend at once, and all three of them pulled at the wand, trying to tug it from the goblin's hand. Unfortunately, the goblin was much stronger. He flicked the wand sharply – and all three fairies went hurtling off the end of it in the direction of the hedge.

"Help!" cried Rachel as she was flung backwards.

Flutter flew out with some of her new butterfly friends. "Are you OK?" she asked, as the three fairies crashed into the leaves.

Kirsty wriggled free. "I'm fine," she said, rather enjoying the soft breeze on her face from Flutter's wing beats. It was actually quite ticklish, she thought…

And then a thought struck her. Hadn't the goblin said that *he* was ticklish? She grinned. "I've just had a great idea!" she said.

Tickle, Tickle!

Kirsty beckoned the butterflies closer and told them her idea. "Do you think you could swarm around the goblin and tickle him with the edges of your wings?" she asked. "If we can get him giggling, he won't be able to concentrate on holding the wand...and hopefully we can grab it!"

Flutter wriggled her wings eagerly.

"Sure!" she said. "That sounds fun. Are the rest of you up for that?"

The other butterflies looked excited too.

"Absolutely!" said Flit. "Let's do it!"

The butterflies flew out of the hedge like a multicoloured stream, and swirled around the goblin, fluttering just close enough to his head and body so that their wing-tips brushed against his skin.

"Oohhh… ooh, that tickles," he spluttered, hunching his shoulders helplessly.

"Hee hee... Ooh! Ha ha ha!"

Soon the goblin was breathless with
giggles, his whole body shaking as he
twisted and turned, trying to get away
from the ticklish butterflies. And
then Rachel
spotted the
wand slip
from his
fingers
and
tumble
to the
ground –
the plan
had worked!

She, Kirsty and
Isabella immediately swooped down
towards the fallen wand.

As soon as Isabella reached out and touched it, it shrank down to its Fairyland size and glowed brightly between her fingers.

"Hurrah!" Isabella cheered, twirling it like a cheerleader's baton. "We did it! Well done, butterflies!"

"Yes, thanks, butterflies, you can stop now," Kirsty called, flying to a safe distance with Isabella and Rachel. "You were wonderful!"

The butterflies fluttered away from the goblin at once and he collapsed onto the floor, still giggling uncontrollably. Then the expression on his face changed to anger as he realised he no longer had the wand. "Hey!" he shouted as he saw it in Isabella's hand. "That's mine!"

"Oh no, it isn't," Isabella retorted. "It's mine — and I'm keeping it. I think it's time you went home now, before anyone spots you!"

The goblin scowled and stomped off, muttering something about not taking orders from silly fairies. Rachel gave a cheer and turned to smile at Kirsty, then noticed her friend was looking at something else. "Is that *Flutter*?" Kirsty asked, puzzled.

Rachel couldn't see the butterfly anywhere at first. She stared at where Kirsty was pointing. "But that's a blue butterfly," she said, confused. "Unless… Flutter, is that really you? You're not grey any more!"

Flutter glanced at her wings and gave a squeak of delight. "I'm blue, I'm blue!" she cried, flying a loop-the-loop in excitement. "Look at my lovely wings!"

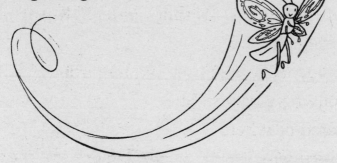

"The grey on Flutter's wings must have been dirt from the pollution in the air," Kirsty realised. "Just like the flowers we saw near the cinema, Rachel."

"Yes, and all that tickling must have brushed off the grey dust," Rachel worked out. She smiled at the happy butterfly. "Now you're even prettier, Flutter!"

Isabella flew over and gave Flutter a little kiss. "Now that I've got my wand, I can start cleaning up the air in this town," she said, "so that no other butterfly ever has to be grey again!" She smiled. "I'll start with the parks and green areas. Trees are brilliant for  absorbing carbon dioxide and turning it into oxygen, which we can breathe. More trees and fewer cars, that's what we need!" Her eyes fell upon the discarded spray cans that were still lying on the ground. "Although first of all, I'm going to do a bit of clearing up right here..."

She waved her wand and a flood of magical blue sparkles swirled out from its tip and onto the cans. Kirsty and Rachel chuckled as, one by one, the cans sailed up into the air and across to the nearest recycling bin, where they dropped inside.

Kirsty, Rachel and the butterflies let out a cheer and Isabella bobbed a little curtsey.

"Thank you, girls, you were brilliant," she said, hugging them each in turn. "And now I should send you back to Seabury. It's nearly time for you to meet your parents."

"Goodbye, Isabella," said Kirsty. "I hope your clean-up magic goes well."

"We'll do what we can to help too," Rachel promised. "Bye!"

Isabella waved her wand and with a whirl of glittering fairy magic, the two girls found themselves in Seabury once again, back to their normal sizes.

They walked towards the cinema to find their parents.

"Wow, look at that!" Kirsty said as a tram went by, heading for the seafront. "I'd love to go on one of those while we're on holiday."

"Much more fun than travelling by car," Rachel said.

"And when we're back at home, I'll ask my teacher if we can do a project about fun ways to come to school, rather than using the car. I must get my old micro-scooter out."

"Or a skateboard would be fun!" Kirsty laughed.

As they drew near the cinema, they could see crowds of people coming out, having just seen a movie there. "That was so exciting!" Kirsty and Rachel heard a boy say to his friend.

The girls exchanged glances. "Not half as exciting as our fairy adventures, I bet!" Rachel whispered with a grin.

Kirsty smiled. "Let's hope we have some more adventures with the Green Fairies very soon!" she said happily.

Now it's time for Rachel and Kirsty to help...

Edie the Garden Fairy

Read on for a sneak peek...

"It's another lovely day, Kirsty!" Rachel exclaimed happily as she and her best friend Kirsty Tate hurried along the winding country lane. The blue sky above them was dotted with fluffy white clouds, and the sun was warm on their faces. "Isn't Rainspell Island just the most *magical* place?"

"I can't think of anywhere else I'd rather go on holiday," Kirsty replied, gazing over the lush green fields. The aquamarine sea sparkled in the distance and seagulls wheeled through the crisp, salty air.

The Tates and the Walkers had arrived on the island three days ago to spend the autumn half-term week there.

"It's great that we're helping to keep Rainspell clean and beautiful, isn't it, Rachel?" Kirsty added. "Do you have the leaflet that came yesterday?"

Rachel pulled the leaflet out of her pocket. *Project Green* was written at the top, and underneath it read:
Would YOU like to make a NEW garden out of an area of disused land? Then please join us at our site in Butterfly Lane tomorrow. Wear old clothes!

"I'm glad we decided to volunteer," Kirsty said, as they studied the leaflet. "We might have our friends the Green Fairies to help us with the environment, but we humans have to do our bit, too!"

Rachel nodded. Rainspell Island was a very special place because it was where she and Kirsty had first become good friends with the fairies. Since then the girls had had many amazing magical adventures while helping the fairies to outwit cold, sly Jack Frost and his goblin servants.

But now it was Rachel and Kirsty's turn to ask the fairies for help. When the girls arrived on Rainspell Island, they'd been shocked to see lots of litter strewn around the golden beach, so they'd asked the King and Queen of Fairyland to help clean up the human world with fairy magic...

Read Edie the Garden Fairy to find out
what adventures are in store for Kirsty and Rachel!

Meet the
Green Fairies

Rachel and Kirsty must rescue the Green Fairies'
magic wands from Jack Frost, before
the environment is damaged!

Meet the fairies, play games
and get sneak peeks at
the latest books!

www.rainbowmagicbooks.co.uk

There's fairy fun for everyone on
our wonderful website.
You'll find great activities, competitions, stories and
fairy profiles, and also a special newsletter.

Get 30% off all Rainbow Magic books at
www.rainbowmagicbooks.co.uk

Enter the code RAINBOW at the checkout.
Offer ends 31 December 2013.

Offer valid in United Kingdom and Republic of Ireland only.

Win Rainbow Magic Goodies!

There are lots of Rainbow Magic fairies, and we want to know which one is your favourite! Send us a picture of her and tell us in thirty words why she is your favourite and why you like Rainbow Magic books. Each month we will put the entries into a draw and select one winner to receive a Rainbow Magic Sparkly T-shirt and Goody Bag!

Send your entry on a postcard to Rainbow Magic Competition, Orchard Books, 338 Euston Road, London NW1 3BH.
Australian readers should email: childrens.books@hachette.com.au
New Zealand readers should write to Rainbow Magic Competition, 4 Whetu Place, Mairangi Bay, Auckland NZ.
Don't forget to include your name and address.
Only one entry per child.

Good luck!

Meet the
Ocean Fairies

Naughty goblins have smashed the magical conch
shell! Kirsty and Rachel must restore it
so that the oceans can have harmony again.

www.rainbowmagicbooks.co.uk